Run, Rabbit, Run!

Written by Mairi Mackinnon

Illustrated by Mark Chambers

D1529644

How this book works

The story of **Run, Rabbit, Run!** has been written for your child to read with your help. Encourage your child to read as much as they can, helping to sound out the words if they get stuck.

I spot six crocs in the park today.

5

There are puzzles after the story, and for these you will need to read the instructions to your child.

You can find out more about helping your child with this book, and with reading in general, on pages 30-31.

Run, Rabbit, Run!

Turn the page to start the story.

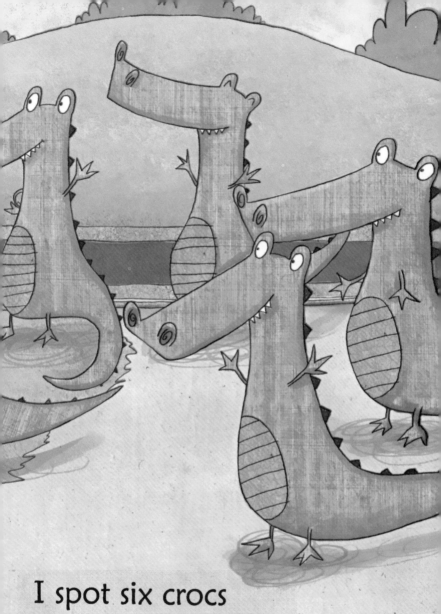

I spot six crocs
in the park today.

"Hey! Play on the train with us," they say.

9

I see seven vultures
high in the sky.

"Ooh, can you fly?
We will help you try!"

"Jump in our boat,
we will go for a row."

“Slow, so slow,
just dip in your toe...”

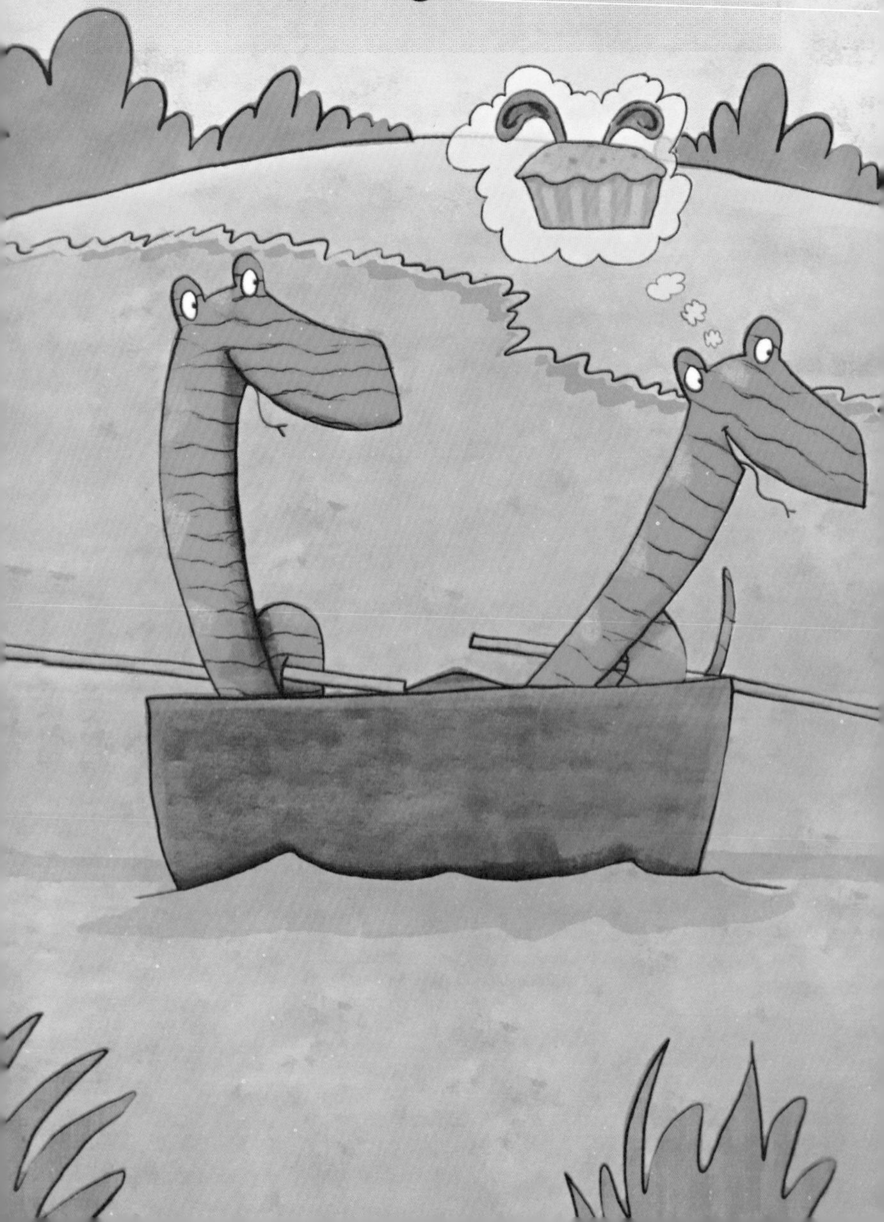

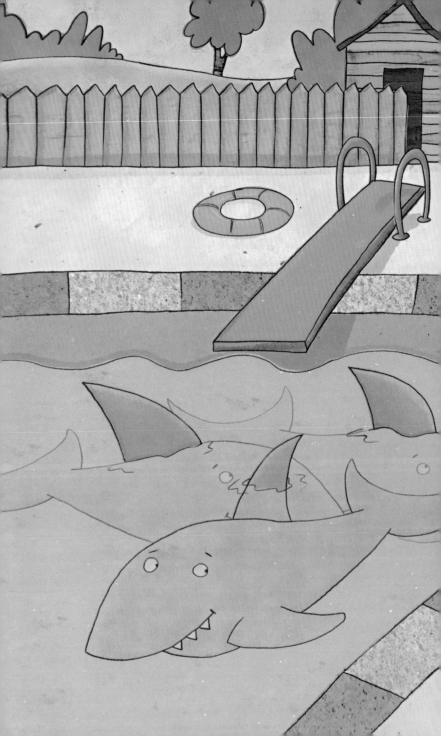

Three sharks swim
in the new blue pool.

"The sun is hot, but you can keep cool."

"Shoo!" I say.
"I am not such a fool."

Puzzle 1

Look at the pictures, then choose
the right sentence for each one.

1.

A "Crayon the train with us."

B "Play on the train with us."

2.

A "Join us for a feast."

B "Join us for a beast."

3.

A "Ooh, can you fly?"

B "Ooh, can you fry?"

4.

A "You can keep cool."

B "You can keep wool."

Puzzle 2

Choose the right speech bubbles for the little animals to warn Rabbit.

1.

2.

3.

Puzzle 3

There is one word in each group that **doesn't** rhyme with the rest. Can you spot it?

1. | hey | fly | play | say |

2. | see | me | tie | tree |

3. | sky | say | high | lie |

4. | too | go | slow | toe |

5. | you | new | row | blue |

Answers to puzzles

Puzzle 1

1. B "Play on the train with us."
2. A "Join us for a feast."
3. A "Ooh, can you fly?"
4. A "You can keep cool."

Puzzle 2

1. "Stay away!"
2. "Better not wait and see!"
3. "That's a lie!"
4. "No! No! No!"

Puzzle 3

1. fly
2. tie
3. say
4. too
5. row

Guidance notes

Usborne Very First Reading is a series of books, specially developed for children who are learning to read. **Run, Rabbit, Run!** is the ninth book in the series, and by this stage your child should be able to read the story alone, with occasional help from you.

The story of **Run, Rabbit, Run!** introduces different spellings of the five sounds shown below:

ai	ee	igh	oa	oo
ay	ea	ie	ow	ew
ey	e	y	oe	ue

Later books in the series gradually introduce more ways of spelling these and other sounds, while reinforcing the ones your child already knows.

You'll find lots more information about the structure of the series, advice on helping your child with reading, extra practice activities and games on the Very First Reading website,* **www.usborne.com/veryfirstreading**

*US readers go to **www.veryfirstreading.com**

Some questions and answers

- **Why do I need to read with my child?**
  Sharing stories makes reading an enjoyable and fun activity for children. It also helps them to develop confidence and stamina. Even if you are not taking an active part in reading, your listening and support are very important.

- **When is a good time to read?**
  Choose a time when you are both relaxed, but not too tired, and there are no distractions. Only read for as long as your child wants to – you can always try again another day.

- **What if my child gets stuck?**
  Don't simply read the problem word yourself, but prompt your child and try to find the right answer together. Similarly, if your child makes a mistake, go back and look at the word together. Don't forget to give plenty of praise and encouragement.

- **We've finished, now what do we do?**
  It's a good idea to read the story several times to give your child more practice and more confidence. Then, when your child is ready, you can go on to the next book in the series, **Late Night at the Zoo.**

Edited by Jenny Tyler and Lesley Sims
Designed by Caroline Spatz

This edition first published in 2013 by Usborne Publishing Ltd.,
Usborne House, 83-85 Saffron Hill, London EC1N 8RT, England.
www.usborne.com Copyright © 2013, 2010 Usborne Publishing Ltd.